MW00897193
Toothless Albert
Written by Carol Taylor
Illustrated by Tracey Moroney

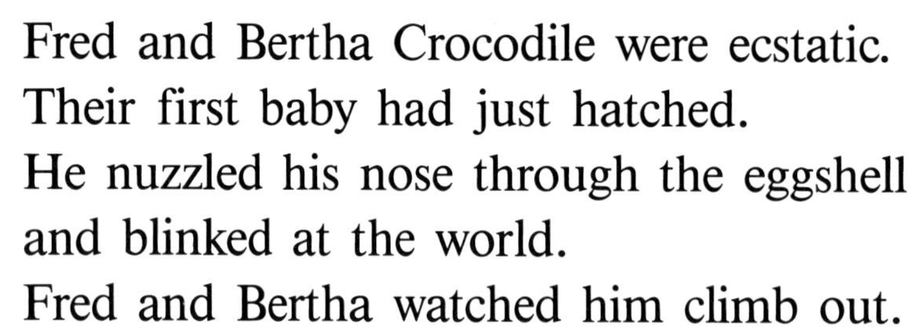

Fred and Bertha Crocodile were ecstatic.
Their first baby had just hatched.
He nuzzled his nose through the eggshell
and blinked at the world.
Fred and Bertha watched him climb out.

"We'll call him Albert," they decided.
"Hi, Albert," they said.
"We're your mom and dad."

Albert smiled.
Fred and Bertha gasped.
They were horrified.
Albert had no teeth!
A crocodile with no teeth.
It was unheard of!

“Poor Albert,” said Bertha.
“All the other crocodiles will make fun of him.”

“He’ll be the local laughing stock,” said Fred.
“Perhaps we could hide him.
Perhaps his teeth will grow soon.”

But it was too late!
The crocodile clan were already
on their way to see the new arrival.

"Look, Albert," said Fred,
"everything will be all right
if you only keep your mouth shut.
Just don't smile or say anything."

Albert tried to do as he was told.
He paraded up and down
showing off his shiny scales
and his fierce-looking jaws.

The other crocodiles were full of
admiration and approval,
until one of the baby crocodiles
cracked a joke.
Albert couldn't help himself.
He laughed.

There was a sudden hush.

“Look at him,” a wily old crocodile said. “He’s got no teeth.”

“Doesn’t he look stupid?” a younger one snorted. “Stupid, toothless Albert!”

The other crocodiles joined the chant. “Toothless Albert! Stupid, toothless Albert!”

Albert hung his head in shame.
He slunk off into the bushes,
dragging his tail behind him.
Fred and Bertha turned their backs
on the cackling crocodiles
and followed Albert.

"Never mind, Albert," said Bertha.
"We love you. But you're going to
find it hard to survive."

Life wasn't easy for Albert.
When he tried to play with the other crocodiles,
they jeered at him, flashing their pearly teeth
and gnashing their jaws.

They gave him the occasional nip,
just to keep him in his place.

When they went out hunting,
Albert lagged behind, snapping at flies,
while the other crocodiles played
'Snare the Snake,' and 'Hunt the Possum.'

Albert often went down to the river
to slurp insects and suck weeds from the water.
He grew to like the taste of seaweed soup.

Bertha was worried.
"Albert will never grow very big," she said.
"Not on mushy food. He needs real meat."

In time, Albert was accepted
by the other crocodiles,
although they never stopped
making fun of him whenever they could.

One day, he noticed that some of the younger crocodiles were losing their teeth.

"Soon they'll be toothless, just like me," he chuckled.

"No, dear," Bertha said. "They're just growing bigger, sharper teeth underneath."

"What happens to the old teeth?" Albert asked.

"The Tooth Fairy collects them," Bertha replied, with a smile.

Albert had an idea.
That night, he wrote a note
to the Tooth Fairy,
and this is what it said:

Dear Tooth Fairy
You have lots of
teeth, and I
have none.
I am very unhappy.
Please could I
have some of your
teeth?
Love Albert xx

Albert put the note under the palm leaves and went to sleep.

In the morning, the note was gone,
and in its place was
the strangest assortment of teeth
Albert had ever seen.

There were long teeth,
short teeth,
old teeth,
new teeth,
shiny teeth,
tiny teeth,
and even some gold-plated teeth.

Albert did his best to put the teeth in order,
but no matter what he did, they looked terrible.

He stuck several in his mouth with glue,
but they wobbled loose and fell out.

Albert was miserable.
He hated being different.
Real crocodile tears trickled
down his scaly face,
and he went down to the river to be alone.

When Bertha was cleaning up the palm leaves
after breakfast, she found all the teeth.
She realized how unhappy Albert was,
and she called Fred.
Together, they thought of a clever plan.
When the Crocodile River Mail came the next day,
they sent off their special request.

Several days later, a package arrived.
After Albert had gone to sleep that night,
his parents placed the package nearby.

As soon as Albert opened his eyes
in the morning, he saw it.
On top was a letter, addressed to Albert.

Albert opened the letter,
and this is what it said:

Dear Albert,
I'm sorry that I didn't get it right the first time.
Hope these will be more to your liking.
Lots of love,
the Tooth Fairy
xxx

Albert carefully unwrapped the package.
He could hardly believe his eyes.
Inside was a set of shiny, sharp,
unique, false crocodile teeth.

They fitted perfectly.

Albert flashed his teeth.
Albert gnashed his jaws.
Albert stretched himself out
and shook his scaly skin.
Albert grinned an evil grin,
and let out a deep crocodile laugh.

Then he went in search of the other crocodiles—
an occasional nip wouldn't do them any harm.